Maleah Wright & Ka

You are limitless and great!
You are special GEMS!
Keep shining! Keep thriving!
HAPPY READING!!

C. Dunbar
~♡~♡~♡~♡~

I Am A Masterpiece.

Yes, That's Me!

Camesha Dunbar

This book is dedicated to my daughter, A'Ryiah

my niece, Jhevonia

my nephew, Ennroy Jr.

my past students

and all the children of the world.

Never forget that you are a masterpiece.

"Where passion and purpose lie, greatness comes alive". C.D

Like the sun I rise very bright.
I stretch my arms wide and I
smile.
I quickly run to the mirror and
there I see someone special,
someone unique.

I see a masterpiece. Yes, that's me.
I am a masterpiece very smart and sweet.

I am brave and bold with lots of colors aglow.
I am fierce and strong.
I conquer and triumph along.
For I am a masterpiece.
Yes, that's me!

I reach for the stars for all can never be lost, there is always hope beyond the dark.
There is always a shining light and a chance to glow.
For I am a masterpiece.
Yes, that's me!

My will is strong for there is a cause.
A cause to shine and a cause to fight for things that are right.

I am fearless and bright, ready to thrive.

I am a masterpiece. Yes, that's me!

LIBRARY

Mopey the
Dolphin

You can catch me at the library having fun with books all day long.

Or you may see me by the art club painting my thoughts on the stand.

Creative and inspired, that's absolutely me.

I am a masterpiece. Yes, that's me!

If you see me by the park, I am happy, wild, and free, twirling and playing in the sunshine that gives me vitamin D.

Free spirited I am and always will be.

For I am a masterpiece. Yes, that's me!

I sing to the tune of my feelings; my jingles keep me on track.
I dance with a beat, for my rhythm never stops.
It keeps me growing, glowing, and going to the place I need to be.
I am a masterpiece. Yes, that's me!

I play my instrument like a star.
I know there are souls to touch and hearts to heal.
Lots of ears to hear the song in me.
For
I am a masterpiece. Yes, that's me!

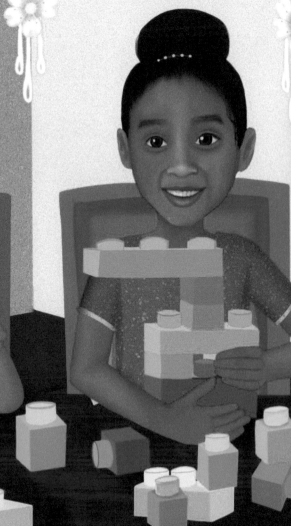

I speak with passion and kindness for I am polite. My heart is pure with so much love to show. I bring out the best in me. For

I am a masterpiece. Yes, that's me!

I have so much depth.
There is much more to me
than what you see.
I am a layer of confidence,
strength, brilliance, and
greatness.
For I am a masterpiece. Yes,
that's me!

I am a light of the world.
I am never afraid of the dark.
I shine through the dark and ignite my light because I am a masterpiece. Yes, that's me!

My adventures are never
ending; they go on and on
and on.
There is so much to discover
and so much to achieve.
I will keep on swaying in the
wind
And be a masterpiece.

Now, hurry to the mirror and there you will see, someone special and someone unique. Yes! That's you - a masterpiece. You too are a masterpiece smart and sweet. Beautifully and wonderfully made, both you and me.

CPSIA information can be obtained
at www.ICGtesting.com
Printed in the USA
BVHW021946210621
609242BV00002B/3